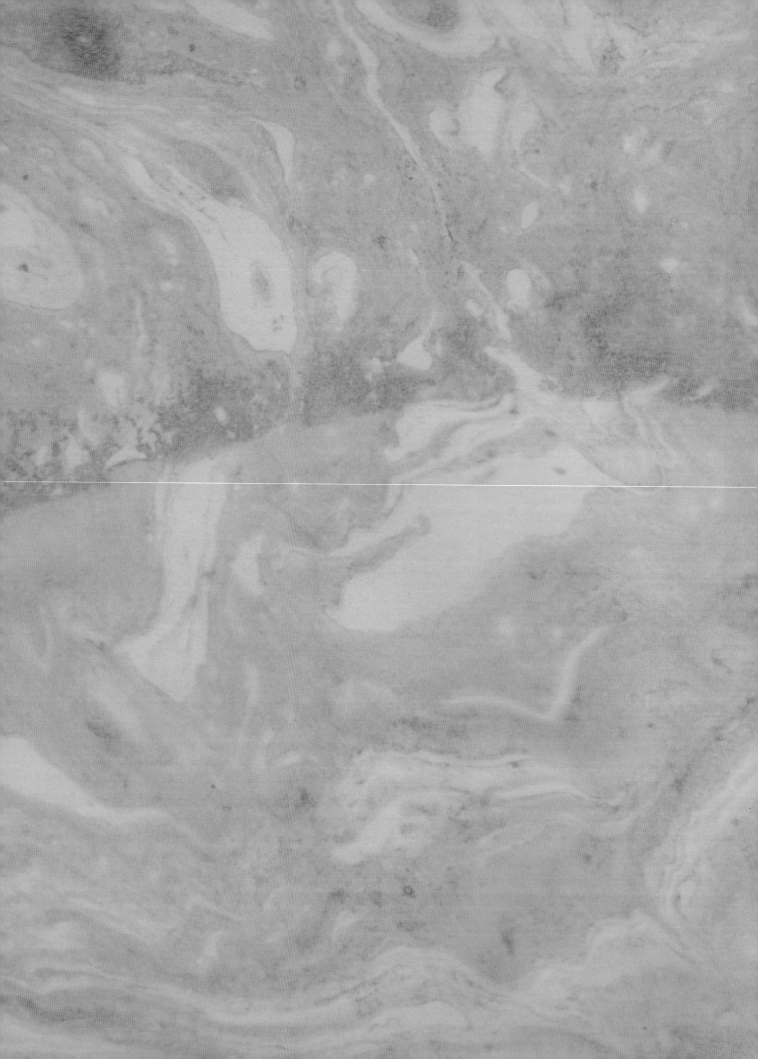

Those Wonderful Antelopes-
The Ēglopes

By

Bobbie Hill

at
Gnomestead
Press
Books&Comics&More
Gnomesteading.com

First Edition
Barbara Hunley Hill
Copyright©2016

ISBN - 13: 978-0-9847436-7-4

Published by

visit www.gnomesteading.com
for other great titles

To All the Children –

for your willingness
to get to know
the wild creatures
and see to their needs!
It's your world,
and you children
often see the best solutions.

These graceful creatures
You see by their pool –
Are elegant Eglopes,
Reddish–gold, as a rule.

O', how they can leap,
They are jumpers of note;
As they bound through the meadows,
They just seem to float.

They graze in the lushness
Of greenish-blue fields,
And nibble the leaves
Of tall trees for their meals.

Now tall trees are Lace trees
Which grow on the plain –
Smell fragrant and sweeter
With each heavy rain.

These are Eglopes' babies
With little pink spots;
Not until they grow tall,
can they eat the Lace tops!

The Eglopes were glad
In their beautiful world
Of clear rippling streams
And pools the wind swirled.

They played many games
Like jump-the-log,
And catch-if-you-can,
And leap-the-frog.

The children from towns
Came to play with Eglopes,
Even rolled down beside them
On cool grassy slopes.

While the boys sailed their boats,
And the girls floated flowers,
The Eglopes munched grass
And lay quietly for hours.

Life was peaceful, so peaceful –
It HAD to remain –
But Man came to survey
That lovely terrain!

10.

It was Man who dug holes
In the great grassy plains,
Built houses and fences
Just for his own gains.

Sadly, the Eglopes
Watched Man dam the streams --
And plow up the meadows,
And fence off their dreams.

They asked themselves, "Why –
Did he chop down the Lace trees?
We've nothing to eat.
Let's do something – Please."

So they jumped into gardens
And ate all the plants,
Even chewed up the laundry –
The shirts and the pants!

And as Eglopes adjusted
To lettuce and parsley,
Man built higher fences,
And Eglopes ate – sparsely!

**Then those noble Eglopes
Lost all of their dignity:
They dug under fences –
That took ingenuity!**

16.

One noise-ridden day
Man was hammering about,
Putting spikes in the ground
To keep Eglopes out.

**Many Eglopes were galloping
To add to the din,
And neighing, and digging
More holes to get IN!**

Soon the wives were whacking
Eglopes with wet sheets
To chase them away
From the carrots and beets.

When above all the ruckus,
Like a firm traffic cop,
The children all lifted their arms
And yelled, "Stop!"

"We don't like this way!
It's a fact; there's no doubt –
We don't want our world
All fenced-in and fenced-out."

"The Eglopes like Lace trees –
And we like them too.
Let's make this a park,
Not a fenced-in old zoo!"

"We like to wade into
The streams that they drink from,
The Eglopes will slide on
The ice we make rinks from."

23.

Man thought and decided:
"The children are right.
We must share our great world,
We now see the light."

So they pulled up the spikes
And took down the fences,
Undammed the streams,
And built some park benches.

They petted the Eglopes
Their children loved so,
And ordered that Lace trees
Be planted to grow...

...into luscious green meals
For the Eglopes' pleasure,
And some miniature Lace trees
For their babies to treasure.

Then the children ran barefoot
Among the bright flowers,
And lifted their faces
To laugh at rain showers.

The Eglopes ate tree tops;
Never bothered the lettuce.
"It's much better," said they,
"When ALL the folks pet us!"

When rainbows formed,
People saw every band.
Now doesn't that seem
Like a happier land?

The End

About the Author

A love of art starts early with a fascination of color, shapes, motion, light and making things with various materials. Bobbie had all those plus a musical, artistic mother who encouraged creativity, which made it possible for those fascinations to grow. By high school she was teaching swimming and dance at beautiful Camp Lochearn on Lake Fairlee in Vermont. After college she drew 3-dimensional engineering views (trimetric projections) for mechanical manuals* until that job was taken over by computers. She became an art teacher and cadette Girl Scout leader in the Catskill Mountains of New York, then Massachusetts. Her two lovable, busy children and her love of the outdoors inspired many of the children's books she has written and illustrated over the years.

* high security clearance work with mechanical drawings for the J63, B52, and Nautilus Submarine

93062743R00024

Made in the USA
Columbia, SC
04 April 2018